Copyright © text and illustrations Century Hutchinson Ltd 1986

First published in 1986 by Hutchinson Children's Books Ltd
An imprint of Century Hutchinson Ltd
Brookmount House, 62-65 Chandos Place, Covent Garden, London WC2N 4NW

Century Hutchinson Publishing Group (Australia) Pty Ltd
16-22 Church Street, Hawthorn, Melbourne, Victoria 3122

Century Hutchinson Group (NZ) Ltd
32-34 View Road, PO Box 40-086, Glenfield, Auckland 10

Century Hutchinson Group (SA) Pty Ltd
PO Box 337, Bergvlei 2012, South Africa

Designed by Sarah Harwood
Edited by Sarah Ware

Set in Stymie Light, by The Keystroke Mill
Printed and bound in Italy

British Library Cataloguing in Publication Data
Hunt, Roderick, *1939-*
Piglet goes to the rescue.
I. Title   II. Gordon, Mike
823'.914[J]   PZ7

ISBN 0 09 167240 6

PIGLET
goes to the
rescue

Written by Rod Hunt
Illustrated by Mike Gordon

Hutchinson
London   Melbourne   Auckland   Johannesburg

Piglet had bad eyesight. In fact, she was short-sighted. This meant she couldn't see things very well until she went up close to them.

Because she couldn't see very well she often made mistakes or did odd things, and that sometimes led to trouble.

The problem was that Piglet didn't know she was short-sighted. Nor did the other animals.

She often passed them without saying hello, because she couldn't see them very well. They would say, 'How rude! We smiled at Piglet but she ignored us.'

Piglet, on the other hand, thought her friends were rude. One day a white plastic bag blew past. She called out, 'Hello Goose!' quite loudly, but it didn't answer.

'That's not very friendly,' she thought. 'I won't speak to Goose again.'

Another day she came across an old brush. She thought it was Hedgehog so she called out, 'Hello! Hello Hedgehog!'

When the brush didn't reply she thought, 'So that's how things are. Well I shan't speak to Hedgehog in future, either.'

Soon Piglet had no friends left. 'I don't know why they're so unfriendly,' she thought. 'I'm sure I don't deserve it.'

The other animals, of course, thought that Piglet was stuck-up. 'We've done nothing to deserve it,' they said.

So Piglet became quite lonely. She began to go for long walks, even though she had often been told never to wander off by herself, and never to go near the dump.

'The dump is a terrible place,' everyone said. 'It's where the rats live.'

Piglet wasn't sure what the dump was. She didn't know where it was either. As for the rats – well, she had never, ever seen one.

Not all rats are nasty, but the ones on the dump were. They were very nasty indeed and the other animals kept well away.

The dump was a place where people threw away all their junk. There were old beds, broken-down fridges, parts of cars, bits of old furniture and lots of horrid rubbish.

The rats scavenged there for food and scraps. The dump was home to them.

One day Piglet was out for a walk, but
being short-sighted she didn't notice a
sign which said 'Keep Out'. She went
straight into the dump, not realising where
she was until she bumped into an old tyre,
a broken lawn-mower and some rusty cans.

'Oh no!' she thought. 'I'm at the dump!' and
she remembered what she had been told.

Then she saw something that made her
heart give an extra beat. A little pig was
standing quite still on the dump amongst
some empty paint cans.

'Hello,' said Piglet, but the little pig didn't reply. 'Ignore me, then,' sniffed Piglet, upset at being snubbed again. But the little pig just stood there looking sad.

'Are you all right?' Piglet asked anxiously. The little pig shook its head.

'You can't stay here,' said Piglet. 'Listen! I can hear the rats. Come back with me.'

The little pig didn't move so Piglet said, 'Are you a prisoner here?' When the little pig's head nodded up and down, Piglet said, 'Then I'll find a way to rescue you.'

Piglet didn't have a plan for rescuing the little pig, but as she ran home she thought, 'If I ask the other animals to help, they'll see that I'm quite nice at heart. And if we rescue the little pig, not only will I have a friend, but the others might like me too.'

She saw a group of animals by the water trough and ran up to them.

'Oh listen, everyone, please,' she panted. 'I've been to the dump. I know I shouldn't have, but I saw a little pig there. He is being held prisoner. Please help me to rescue him.'

The animals looked at Piglet in amazement. They were not used to her speaking, so what she said now came as a shock.

'The dump of all places,' began Hen.

'Please don't be cross,' begged Piglet, 'You must help before it's too late.'

'If Piglet has found a fellow animal in danger,' said Goose, 'then it's our duty to help – rats or no rats. But how?'

'Ask Dog,' said Goat wisely. 'The rats are scared of Dog. Right, Piglet, lead on! We'll call for Dog on the way.'

Dog and Piglet led the animals past the sign saying 'Keep Out' and into the dump.

'What a horrid place,' cried Hen. 'I hope we don't meet any rats.'

But as she spoke the rats appeared from nowhere and stood glaring nastily at the animals with their beady red eyes.

'Well, what do you want?' demanded the biggest rat, showing off his sharp teeth.

'We don't want trouble,' said Dog. 'Just give us the little pig you've captured.'

'Captured a pig!' said the rat scornfully. He threw back his head and laughed aloud at the bewildered animals.

'Here's your pig,' said the rat, as the others dragged out an old plastic piggy bank. Its broken head nodded with the wind.

Poor short-sighted Piglet! She hadn't seen that the little pig was only a broken toy. She went hot with embarrassment.

'Piglet, if this is your idea of a joke, it's not funny,' said Goose acidly.

'You've made fools of us all in front of the rats,' said Goat, with a sniff.

'To say nothing of the waste of my most valuable time,' put in Dog.

'She should get her eyes tested,' sneered the big rat. 'She needs glasses.'

'We've got a pair somewhere,' said a rat. He scrambled among the rubbish and dragged out a huge pair of spectacles.

'Make her try them on,' called Hen.

Goose picked up the glasses in her beak and put them on Piglet's nose. Then everyone laughed including the rats.

But Piglet cried, 'Why, these glasses are wonderful. I can see things I've never seen before. What lovely feathers Hen has!'

Hen blushed and all the animals felt ashamed because they had laughed at Piglet's glasses.

It had never occurred to them that she couldn't see very well. Now they understood why she had ignored them when they walked past.

'We're sorry, Piglet,' they said.

Piglet said she was sorry, too. Now with her glasses, life was quite different.

'Being able to see properly is wonderful. I never realised how beautiful everything is,' she said happily. 'But best of all, I can see that all the animals are my friends.'